Disney · PIXAR

INCREDIBLES 2
Read-Along
STORYBOOK AND CD

The Incredibles face their biggest challenge yet—stopping a criminal mastermind and convincing a wary public that Supers should be legal again. You can read along with me in your book. You will know it's time to turn the page when you hear this sound. . . .
Let's begin now.

Printed in the United States of America
First Paperback Edition, May 2018
1 3 5 7 9 10 8 6 4 2
Library of Congress Control Number: 2017942202
ISBN 978-1-368-01194-5
For more Disney Press fun, visit www.disneybooks.com

Disney PRESS
Los Angeles • New York

SUSTAINABLE FORESTRY INITIATIVE
Certified Sourcing
www.sfiprogram.org
SFI-00993
Logo Applies to Text Stock Only

Municiberg was under attack! The diabolical villain known as the Underminer was using a gigantic tunneler to dig under a full city block. When the buildings collapsed, the Underminer cleaned out all the bank vaults on that street! Mr. Incredible tried to stop him, but the Underminer escaped.

The out-of-control tunneler then exploded through the surface and hit the monorail tracks. In an instant, Frozone formed an ice bridge to redirect the train and save the passengers.

Elastigirl jumped on the tunneler and opened the hatch. "We have to stop this thing before it gets to the overpass!"

As she climbed inside, Mr. Incredible had a terrible realization. "It's headed for city hall!"

The Supers worked fast to knock out the tunneler's engine. The machine lurched and ground to a halt on the steps of city hall, just inches from the door.

The Incredibles thought the police would thank them for trying to stop the Underminer, but instead, they were blamed for causing all the damage.

Mr. Incredible couldn't believe what he was hearing. "We didn't start this fight!"

That was true, but the police were mad that the Underminer had gotten away and the city was a wreck. If the Supers had captured the villain, things would be different.

Elastigirl sighed. "So, you support us . . . as long as we win?"

The officer shook his head. The police did not and would not officially support Supers.

The Incredibles' friend, Agent Rick Dicker, dropped the Parr family off at a motel. He said the government program that protected the Supers was being shut down. The agency would cover the motel room for two weeks, but after that, the Parrs would be on their own.

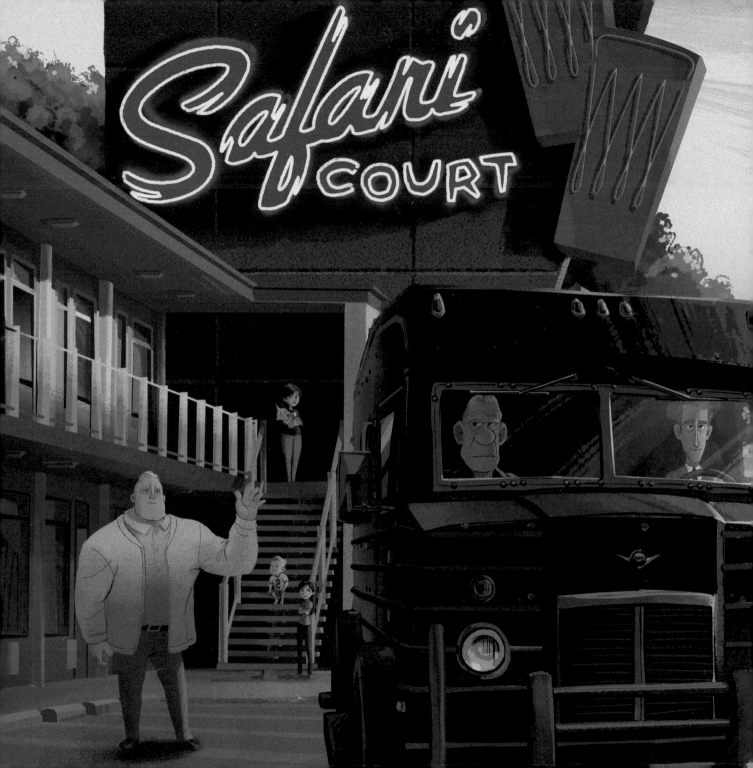

No longer Superheroes, Helen and Bob were out of work.

But their friend Lucius, the Super known as Frozone, said he'd met a business tycoon who wanted to help Supers become legal again. The three friends went to see Winston Deavor, the head of a high-tech company called DevTech. He had a personal reason for wanting to help them: his parents died as a result of a robbery, and he thought Supers could have stopped it.

"If we want to change people's perceptions about Superheroes, we need *you* to share your perceptions with the world!"

Elastigirl was puzzled. "How do we do that?"

Winston's tech genius sister, Evelyn, explained that a tiny camera sewn into each Supersuit would stream their heroic acts to screens everywhere.

Winston grinned. "You just be Super, and we'll get the public on your side, and we won't stop until you're all legal again."

Everybody loved the idea. Winston wanted Elastigirl to go on the first mission. Mr. Incredible was disappointed, but he was happy for Elastigirl.

"You'll be great. I'll watch the kids—no problem. Easy."

Winston arranged for the Parr family to move into one of his lavish homes.

The house was amazing, but Violet thought it was over the top. "Good thing we won't stand out. Wouldn't want to attract any unnecessary attention."

Dash, on the other hand, thought it was paradise. "It's got a big yard. Near a forest! And a pool!"

Meanwhile, Helen found a gift basket in her bedroom with a note from Evelyn . . . and a new Supersuit. The note said there was an accessory to her suit in the garage. It was a jet-powered, all-electric Elasticycle! Helen hopped on the super bike, ready for action.

"You will be great."

"I *will* be great. And you will, too." Elastigirl smiled and opened the throttle.

After only one day of parenting on his own, Bob was frazzled. The kids had endless demands!

First Violet was getting ready to go on a movie date, and Bob insisted on a curfew.

"I want you back here by ten thirty."

"Eleven-ish?"

"Ten-ish, heading for nine thirty-ish!"

"Ten thirty-ish it is. Sheesh!"

Then Jack-Jack needed a bedtime story to help him fall asleep.

"In the county of Noddoff, the Frubbers of Freep are all giving in to the sweet succor of sleep. . . ."

It worked. Bob put Jack-Jack in his crib and was ready to nod off himself.

But Dash needed help with his homework. Bob was stumped.

"Why would they change math? Math is math!"

"Ehh, it's okay, Dad. I'll just wait for Mom to get back."

Elastigirl was busy waiting for crime in a dark alleyway. The Elasticycle had a built-in police scanner so she could react quickly to any crimes being committed. While she waited, Elastigirl watched the mayor of New Urbem dedicate a new superfast hovertrain. After the ribbon-cutting ceremony, the train rose up off the tracks and raced out of the station *backward*!

Elastigirl took off after the train, pushing her Elasticycle to well over two hundred miles per hour! Her suitcam broadcast everything in real time. She jumped onto the roof of the train, made her way inside, and quickly found the train's brake. The train stopped just seconds from total disaster!

Elastigirl checked on the passengers. "Is everybody all right? Is anybody injured?"

Luckily, the guests were unhurt. Elastigirl rushed to the crew cab, where she discovered the train's engineer had no idea what had happened. It was like he had been in a trance.

Oddly, a message for Elastigirl popped up on the train's control panel:

WELCOME BACK, ELASTIGIRL. —THE SCREENSLAVER

Later that night, after putting Jack-Jack into his crib, Bob sat on the couch and fell right to sleep. As he snoozed, the baby came downstairs and roamed around the house.

Jack-Jack heard a noise coming from outside. Through the patio door, he could see a raccoon raiding the family garbage can. It looked like the animal was wearing a mask, like a robber! Without hesitation, Jack-Jack passed *right through* the glass door and challenged the raccoon. The critter lunged at Jack-Jack. The baby fought back by shooting laser beams out of his eyes! The raccoon dodged every blast. Suddenly, Jack-Jack *multiplied* and surrounded the pest!

Bob woke up to all the commotion and ran outside. He was astounded and proud.

"You . . . have . . . powers! Yeah, baby! And there's not a scratch on you!"

Meanwhile, the heroic story of how Elastigirl stopped the runaway train was all over the news. Winston set up a television interview, and now she was being interviewed by the famous TV anchorman Chad Brentley. But seconds into the program, the newsman's teleprompter was taken over by hypnotic light patterns. Brentley began reading new text off the prompter like a robot. Someone was speaking through him! The message warned the TV audience that they could easily be entranced and controlled through any screen. Behind it all was an evil genius who called himself the Screenslaver!

To prove his power, the Screenslaver said he would bring down a helicopter that was flying over the city with a foreign ambassador on board!

Elastigirl sprang into action. She ran, jumped, stretched, and swung across the city skyline until she reached the ambassador's helicopter.

"Ambassador! We're too low to parachute! We're gonna have to slingshot—hang on! Trust me!" Elastigirl quickly grabbed the ambassador— just before another helicopter sliced through the chopper in midair. She brought everyone safely to the ground.

Elastigirl was a hero, and Winston was thrilled! It was time to push for making Supers legal.

"We're going to have a summit at sea. We'll gather leaders and Supers from all over the world!"

Elastigirl was glad things were going well, but something was bothering her. "I didn't get him. Screenslaver is still out there!"

She told Evelyn she had a plan to capture the villain by tracking his broadcast signal. She just needed a device that could do it. Evelyn said she'd help create a new tech contraption to help.

During Elastigirl's next interview with Chad Brentley, the Screenslaver cut in again.

As he rambled on, Elastigirl tracked the signal and found his lair. Suddenly, Screenslaver came through the door!

Elastigirl tried to take off his flickering goggles, but the Screenslaver escaped. He ran onto the roof and jumped! Elastigirl stretched herself into a parachute and held on to him as they fell. As they floated to the ground, the building exploded! Elastigirl pulled off her captive's mask. The young man behind it said he had no idea what had just happened!

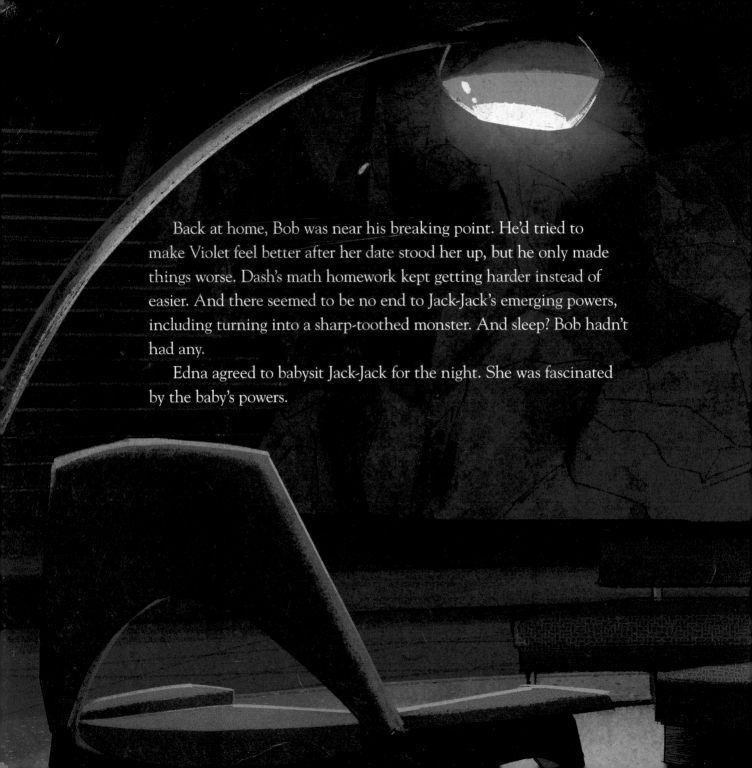

Back at home, Bob was near his breaking point. He'd tried to make Violet feel better after her date stood her up, but he only made things worse. Dash's math homework kept getting harder instead of easier. And there seemed to be no end to Jack-Jack's emerging powers, including turning into a sharp-toothed monster. And sleep? Bob hadn't had any.

Edna agreed to babysit Jack-Jack for the night. She was fascinated by the baby's powers.

When Bob got back to the house, he looked more tired than ever. "I'm used to knowing what the right thing to do is, but now I'm not sure anymore. I just want to be . . . a good dad."

Violet wrapped her arms around her dad. "You're not good. You're Super."

Bob grinned and fell right to sleep. Seventeen hours later, he felt like himself again!

A party celebrating Elastigirl's success was in full swing. In a few hours, world leaders were going to legalize Supers at a ceremony aboard the DevTech yacht.

While everyone cheered, Elastigirl watched slow-motion video of the Screenslaver's lair, shot from her suitcam. Something wasn't right. She found the editing room and took a closer look at the footage. Not long after, Evelyn joined her.

"Look at that. One of Screenslaver's monitors is tuned in to my suitcam. Isn't the suitcam closed-circuit?"

Evelyn said it was. "Maybe he hacked it? Maybe he wanted you to find him."

Still, things weren't adding up. It was too easy. "Wait. All Screenslaver needs to do to hypnotize someone is get a screen in front of their eyes."

Elastigirl looked at the hypno-goggles she'd pulled off the Screenslaver. Mini screens were built into the lenses! The guy she'd captured wasn't the Screenslaver—he was being *controlled* by the Screenslaver!

"You are good." Evelyn quickly put the hypno-goggles over Elastigirl's eyes. Hypnotic lights flashed, and instantly, Elastigirl was thrust into a trance.

When the hypno-goggles stopped flashing, Elastigirl regained her senses. She tried to move, but it was painful. Evelyn had locked her in a subzero computer room to keep Elastigirl from using her power. It was so cold that if she tried to stretch, she'd break!

Elastigirl glared at Evelyn. "So you're the Screenslaver. I counted on you!" She asked why Evelyn betrayed her and Winston.

Evelyn believed the public—including her own family—was better off without Supers.

Elastigirl knew she was in danger. "Are you gonna kill me?"

Evelyn smirked and said no. She wanted to use her instead. With control of Elastigirl, Evelyn would make Supers illegal forever. The hypno-goggles lit up, and Elastigirl was once again under the Screenslaver's control.

With Elastigirl neutralized, Evelyn set about capturing the rest of the Incredibles. She phoned Bob and lured him to the DevTech yacht by telling him Elastigirl was in trouble.

"I'll be there in fifteen minutes!"

Bob called Frozone to watch the kids and sped off. Minutes later, six Supers wearing hypno-goggles showed up to take the kids to DevTech. They were under the Screenslaver's control, too.

Luckily, Frozone arrived and quickly blocked the door with a wall of ice. But the hypnotized Supers broke through and went after Dash and Violet.

"What's going on?!"

"RUN!"

Violet used a force field as they ran for Frozone's car. But a Super named Reflux blocked their path with lava, and another crushed the vehicle!

The fight continued in the house until, suddenly, the Incredibile burst through the living room! Dash had summoned it with the remote. The kids escaped just as the Supers overtook Frozone and slapped a pair of hypno-goggles over his eyes. They were taking him to Evelyn Deavor.

When Mr. Incredible arrived at the ship, Evelyn made Elastigirl put hypno-goggles on him, too.

With Elastigirl, Frozone, and Mr. Incredible now under her control, Evelyn commanded the hypnotized trio to steer the boat toward land and smash the controls. The ship was on course to crash into the city!

Luckily, the kids had ordered the Incredibile to take them to the DevTech ship so they could help their parents. When they found them, Jack-Jack floated over to Elastigirl and removed her hypno-goggles. Realizing what had happened, Elastigirl took the goggles off Mr. Incredible and Frozone.

"Evelyn Deavor controls the Screenslaver, and until a second ago—us!"

Evelyn watched the scene unfold from her control room. She commanded the hypnotized Supers to attack. While Mr. Incredible and a Super named Brick threw punches, another Super named Voyd opened a vortex in front of Elastigirl. But she reached through it and pulled off Voyd's hypno-goggles. One Super shot electricity at Violet, but Jack-Jack snuck up on him and ripped off his goggles, too. Soon all the Supers were released from the Screenslaver's control.

The ship was still headed for destruction, and Evelyn was trying to escape in a jet! Voyd opened a portal for Elastigirl and transported her into the cockpit. Evelyn made the jet climb, dive, and spin to try and throw Elastigirl from the plane, but her plan backfired. Elastigirl took control of the jet and directed it to hit one of the ship's hydrofoils. Right before impact, she grabbed Evelyn and ejected out of the plane. With Voyd's help, they landed on the deck of the ship.

The Incredibles gave up trying to slow the ship down. Their only hope was to turn the boat away from the city. Mr. Incredible knew what he needed to do.

"Dash, I am going to the rudder. Once I turn the ship, you hit the pull-up button."

"Okay, Dad. Got it!

Mr. Incredible used every ounce of his strength to turn the jammed rudder. When Dash brought Mr. Incredible back to the surface, he was gasping for air. At the same time, Frozone created a wall of ice between the ship and the city.

With moments to spare, the ship came to a stop before hitting the Municiberg waterfront. Everyone on board was safe!

And at last, the real Screenslaver was in custody.

Greeted as heroes by the city's grateful citizens, the Supers finally achieved their goal. A judge thanked them for their extraordinary service and fully restored the legal status of Superheroes.

The Supers cheered. Elastigirl put her arms around Mr. Incredible and Frozone and smiled. "You guys got the next shift. I'm beat!"